THE SWISS FAMILY ROBINSON

Library of Congress Cataloging-in-Publication Data

James, Raymond.
    Swiss family Robinson / by Johann Wyss; retold by Raymond James;
illustrated by Ellen Beier.
       p.   cm.—(Troll illustrated classics)
    Summary: Relates the fortunes of a shipwrecked family as they
imaginatively adapt to life on an island with abundant animal and
plant life.
    ISBN 0-8167-1875-X (lib. bdg.)   ISBN 0-8167-1876-8 (pbk.)
    [1. Survival—Fiction. 2. Family life—Fiction.] I. Beier,
Ellen, ill. II. Wyss, Johann David, 1743-1818. Schweizerische
Robinson. III. Title.
PZ7.J1543Sw 1990
[Fic]—dc20   89-33888

Printed in the United States of America.
10 9 8 7 6 5 4 3 2

THE SWISS FAMILY ROBINSON

JOHANN WYSS

Retold by
Raymond James

Illustrated by
Ellen Beier

Troll Associates

The sky cracked open, and for seven days a terrible storm raged at sea. The ship carrying the Robinson family tossed like a top. Huge waves battered the sides. Leaks sprung up everywhere. The masts had been split by lightning and the sails ripped by the howling wind. The ship was blown far off course and was in uncharted waters. It was also in immediate danger of sinking.

"Be brave, children," said Mr. Robinson to his four sons below deck. Fritz, the oldest at fifteen, nodded. The other three boys, thirteen-year-old Ernest, ten-year-old Jack, and seven-year-old Franz, tried to stay calm. But their fear increased as the wind and rain outside increased. Even Mrs. Robinson shot a frightened look at her husband.

Then, amid the roar of the waves crashing against the boat, the Robinsons heard two shrill cries. "Land, land!" was the first, followed a minute later by "Lower away, men!"

Mr. Robinson and Fritz dashed up on deck. From there, they saw the last lifeboat pulling away. The captain and crew were abandoning ship!

Mr. Robinson shouted after them and waved his arms to try to get them to return for his family. But it was no use. The lifeboat slipped off into the foaming sea, leaving the Robinsons behind. They were the only humans left on board the ship.

A sudden jolt knocked Mr. Robinson and Fritz to the deck. The ship had rammed between two large rocks jutting out of the sea. Fritz and his father could see the faint outline of a rocky coast about three miles away. It was land, all right. But how would they get there without a lifeboat?

Mr. Robinson and his oldest son rejoined the rest of the family below deck. With as much courage as he could muster, Mr. Robinson said, "We're the only ones left. The captain and crew have taken the last boat. Our only chance is to sit out the storm here." He paused, looking at the troubled faces of his family. "Let's try to get some rest now. We'll need our strength in the morning." But try as they might, none of the Robinsons could sleep a wink that night.

The next morning, the storm began to taper off. Soon only a stiff breeze and a light mist remained. The waves were calm. And in the distance, the rocky shore of an island could be seen.

"Now," said Mr. Robinson, thinking out loud, "how *do* we get ashore? Swimming is out of the question. Any ideas?"

Each boy turned and looked at the others. Then Fritz spoke up. "How about a raft, Father?"

6

"I don't think we could make a raft strong enough to carry all of us safely to shore, Fritz," he replied. "No, we need something else."

"Father," said Jack, "can't we all get into a big tub and just float there? Remember how I used the old wooden bathtub to sail around the pond back home?"

Mr. Robinson snapped his fingers. "Why, Jack, I think you have something there. Those four big casks in the hold— let's bring them up on deck. I have an idea."

The four boys and their father went down to the ship's hold. Together, they managed to get the four heavy casks up on deck. There, Mr. Robinson turned them on their sides and sawed each one in half. Then he placed them close together in a single row by the water's edge. He nailed a long plank to the bottoms of the eight halves. Two other planks were nailed to their sides and a rope attached to one end. The other end of the rope was tied to part of the ship's railing that had not broken away.

Carefully, father and sons pushed the casks into the water. They floated, though at a sharp angle. Mr. Robinson took some empty brandy jugs and corked their tops. Then he tied the jugs to the casks to balance them.

"All right," he said, smiling for the first time in eight days, "let's get some supplies from the ship. Then we'll be off."

The family collected canvas to make a tent, a chest of carpenter's tools, rifles, pistols, gunpowder, bullets, knives, fishing rods and tackle, an iron pot, plant seeds, and two cases of dried soup and biscuits. All were put into the two floating casks that would not be carrying family members. Just as they were about to climb in the casks and shove off with the paddles they'd found in the hold, a loud noise rose up from below deck.

"The hens and roosters!" cried young Franz. "Father, please take them with us." The ducks and geese on board had been set free to fend for themselves. And of the cow, donkey, two dogs, and hens and roosters remaining, Franz was especially fond of the latter.

"Stay here," said Mr. Robinson. "I'll get them." He climbed out of his cask, went below deck, and returned with a canvas bag squirming in his hands. He then gently dumped the contents into one of the supply casks. The hens clucked and the roosters crowed as he placed a wire mesh over the top of the cask. "We'll come back for the other animals when we can," Mr. Robinson said.

At last, the Robinsons were off, dipping their paddles into the water as they headed the casks toward shore. A couple of loud splashes from behind, however, made them turn their heads around. The two dogs, Juno and Turk, had just dived in after them. They swam right behind the casks, every so often resting their paws on the floating brandy jugs.

8

Once on shore, the Robinson family unloaded the supplies, set free the hens and roosters, and let the two dogs run loose. The four brothers then fanned out to collect wood for a fire. As they did, Mr. Robinson used the canvas to set up a tent on the beach. But no sooner had he pegged the sides of the canvas into the sand than he heard Jack crying for help. Grabbing a hatchet, Mr. Robinson ran toward a pool of water where Jack was standing. There, he saw Jack's leg caught in the powerful claw of a huge lobster.

Mr. Robinson whacked the lobster with the blunt side of his hatchet. The lobster loosened its grip enough so that Jack could remove his leg from its claw. Mr. Robinson took hold of the lobster and flung it on the dry sand. Jack raced over, picked up the dead lobster, and ran toward his mother.

''Mother, Mother, look!'' Jack shouted gleefully. ''We can have lobster soup for supper!'' Mrs. Robinson merely rolled her eyes.

''Has anyone seen Fritz?'' asked Mr. Robinson. In the commotion over the lobster, Fritz had wandered off. He was nowhere in sight.

''Fritz! Fritz!'' the family began to shout.

Then, from a great distance down the beach, the oldest boy shouted back. To his parents and brothers, he looked no bigger than an ant moving along the sand. It was many minutes before his family could see that he was walking toward them, holding his hands behind his back.

''Fritz, you must stay with the others for now,'' warned his father. ''We have no idea who or what may be on this island with us. We simply can't have everyone going off alone without permission. Do you understand, son?''

"Yes, sir," replied Fritz. He took his hands from behind his back. In them was the body of a small, wild pig.

"Excellent, Fritz, excellent!" exclaimed his mother. "Between the pig you caught and the lobster that caught Jack, er, the lobster that Jack caught, we'll have a fine supper indeed."

With the wood the boys had collected, the fire was now burning brightly. Over it Mrs. Robinson cooked supper. It was every bit as good as she had promised. The entire family ate with hearty appetites. And Jack eagerly lapped up the lobster soup she served, and asked for another helping.

An hour after supper, night came. The children were surprised at how quickly darkness fell on them.

"We must be close to the equator," said Mr. Robinson. "That would explain why night comes on so suddenly. Let's go inside the tent and get some sleep. There's nothing more we can do now anyway."

"Should we stand guard, Father?" asked Fritz as the others entered the tent.

"Juno and Turk will tell us if trouble approaches," he answered. The two dogs were lying by the still-glowing embers of the fire. "Come on, son. Let's get some sleep."

10

The next morning, after a quick breakfast, Mr. Robinson and Fritz started to explore the shore of the island. Only a few hundred yards of sand separated the ocean from steep, sheer cliffs. Without some entrance through these cliffs, they knew the family would not be able to travel inland.

Fritz and his father walked across a stream and headed toward a wood. There, a grove of immense trees grew. What was unusual about these trees was that their thick roots arched above the ground and supported the wide trunk in the air. The heavy branches began about thirty feet up the trunk. One tree had two branches about twenty feet apart and level with each other. A third branch was centered about ten feet above these two branches.

"Father," said Fritz, "are you thinking what I'm thinking?"

"A tree house!" replied Mr. Robinson. "We could make it with some sailcloth and planks from the ship. Let's get back and tell the others, Fritz."

But as father and son wheeled around to return, a fig dropped nearby. Then another fell closer to them, followed by still another. Fritz looked up the trunk of the tree and saw some monkeys swinging in the high branches. He took his rifle and aimed it at them, but his father ordered him to stop.

"No, Fritz," said Mr. Robinson. "Those monkeys may prove more useful to us alive than dead."

Fritz had a puzzled look on his face. "What do you mean, Father?"

"Why don't you throw some pebbles up into the tree and find out?" he said.

Fritz took a handful of sand pebbles and tossed them high into the tree. A few seconds later, figs rained down on them, just missing their heads.

"Why should we climb up and pick the fruit when the monkeys will do the job for us?" said Mr. Robinson.

The two of them gathered up as many figs as they could and stuffed them into their pockets. Then they started back. They recrossed the stream and had come within sight of the tent when they saw Turk suddenly leap into a group of monkeys huddled below a tree. The monkeys were completely taken by surprise. Turk attacked one of the monkeys carrying a baby on her back. Fritz and his father ran toward the scene but arrived too late. The mother lay dead.

The baby, however, rushed toward Fritz and climbed up his body, flinging its arms around his neck. Turk snarled from below as Fritz ran about, trying to pry the baby monkey's paws from his neck. But the more Fritz tried to free himself, the tighter the monkey held on. Finally, Mr. Robinson grabbed Turk by his furry neck and sat him down on the sand, and the baby monkey let itself be cradled in Fritz's arms.

"Can we keep him, Father?" asked Fritz. The baby monkey's eyes widened in fear as Turk continued to growl. Its tiny paws clung to Fritz's shirt sleeve.

"We'll have to ask your mother," replied Mr. Robinson.

When the two approached the tent, Ernest, Jack, and Franz ran toward Fritz. Mrs. Robinson stood in front of the tent, watching her sons pet the monkey Fritz was holding. She looked at her husband, who shrugged his shoulders and smiled.

"One more animal can't hurt," he said softly. His wife, seeing young Franz stroke the baby monkey's head, nodded. "We have good news, too," said Mr. Robinson. "Fritz and I found a perfect place for us to live. In a tree!"

Mrs. Robinson's jaw dropped. "You don't mean to tell me that you expect all of us to live like birds, do you?"

"The idea isn't as far-fetched as you may think," her husband replied. "High above the beach, we'd be safe from any prowling animals. And we wouldn't have to rely on the dogs or ourselves to keep watch. If you agree, Fritz and I will take the casks out to the ship to get the materials we'll need. And we'll bring back the donkey and the cow."

With Mrs. Robinson's approval, Fritz and his father did just that. Out on the wreck, they collected planks, nails, sailcloth, and other supplies, placing them in six of the casks. Then they tied empty wooden kegs on each side of the donkey and the cow and tied the animals loosely together by a long rope around their necks. Carefully, father and son pushed the two animals into the water. They submerged, then popped up with a splash.

With one end of the rope in his hand, Mr. Robinson got into his cask. Then Fritz jumped into his and pushed the casks off with his foot. They began paddling back to shore with the donkey and the cow trailing behind them.

With some of the planks, Mr. Robinson and his four sons built a crude bridge across the stream. This would give the donkey and the cow surer footing. It would also make it easier to haul supplies from the tent to the new home they were going to build in the tree.

The first problem in building the tree house was getting up to the lower branches. Mr. Robinson had an idea. He cut two long pieces of rope, trimmed some bamboo stalks, and made a rope ladder. Then both he and Fritz tossed one end of the ladder over a lower branch. As Mr. Robinson held one end, Fritz climbed up. Sitting on the branch, Fritz fastened the ladder securely. It was now ready for use.

The family climbed up and down the ladder as they worked on the tree house. The floor was a crosshatching of planks nailed together across the two level branches. On either side of the floor was a wall made of planks that rose about head high. Sailcloth was draped over the center branch above and then tied to the lower branches. The rear of the house was set against the trunk of the tree, so the only opening was in the front. Mrs. Robinson cut buttonholes into one front flap of the sailcloth and sewed buttons along the other. They now had an entranceway they could shut at night and in bad weather. The tree house was finished.

As evening came, the family hauled up what pieces of furniture and bedding they could squeeze into their new home thirty feet in the air. Snug inside, the boys insisted on naming landmarks. Their previous home on the beach was called Tentholm. The islet in the bay where they saw gray fins knifing through the water was called Shark Island. The marsh where the bamboo grew was called Flamingo Marsh because of the great number of flamingos wading there. The stream was called Jackal River because of some wild yellow jackals Turk and Juno sniffed and chased off there. And Falconhurst was the name the boys gave to their new home in the tree.

Getting ready for bed, Mr. Robinson suggested he and Fritz return one last time to the wreck the following morning. They would collect the remainder of the ship's supplies before another storm could sink the vessel for good. Mrs. Robinson offered to stay behind and plant a garden. The other three boys volunteered to hunt and fish while their father and older brother were out at the wreck. Then Mrs. Robinson went over to button the front flaps of the entrance. Amid a chorus of good-nights, the Robinson family settled in for a sound sleep above the ground.

The sun was still rising when Mr. Robinson and Fritz boarded the wreck. It had taken on more water since the last time they visited it. Mr. Robinson knew it wouldn't stay afloat much longer.

Quickly, the two rounded up a copper boiler, iron plates, a small barrel of gunpowder, and a couple of wheelbarrows. These were put in the casks. Fritz was searching the hold for anything he might have overlooked when he noticed something wedged between two partitions. On closer inspection, he saw the parts for a small boat packed away there. Fritz called to his father.

"What is it, Fritz?" Mr. Robinson asked.

"Look!" said Fritz, pointing.

Mr. Robinson examined the area his son was pointing at. "It's a pinnace!" exclaimed Mr. Robinson.

"A what?" blurted Fritz, scratching his head.

"A pinnace. It's a small craft used to transport people between ships at sea. If we can put it together, we'll find it a lot sturdier than those casks we've been using. Let's get it out from between these partitions."

They took the parts out slowly. Some of them were very heavy. In fact, the weight of the pinnace's hull was too heavy for Fritz and his father to carry up on deck.

"We'll assemble it right here in the hold," said Mr. Robinson. "Afterward, I can set a small explosive on the wood outside. With luck, it'll blow a hole big enough for the pinnace to slip through undamaged."

Side by side, father and son worked on the small craft. It was hard work. But finally they had the boat assembled, mounting two small brass guns on either side of its bow.

Back up on deck, Mr. Robinson and Fritz got into the casks and paddled around to the outside of the ship's hold. Mr. Robinson set the charge and lit a long fuse. The flame sizzled as it traveled slowly down the fuse. Father and son rapidly paddled a safe distance away. Then they waited.

Suddenly, there was a loud explosion. Wood fragments flew and hissed into the water. A billow of smoke rose up from the ship's side. When it cleared, a gaping hole remained. Fritz and his father paddled closer. They could see that the pinnace was not damaged. The wreck, however, was now taking on a lot of water. They didn't have much time.

"Stay here in the casks, Fritz," ordered his father. "I'll climb below and see if I can push the pinnace through the hole."

Fritz waited. More and more water rushed into the hold. The ship groaned under the pressure. Fritz was worried about his father. Would he be able to get the pinnace out in time? Would *he* get out in time?

Fritz saw the pinnace inching forward toward the water. Then it fell to the waves below with a short slap and was sailing freely on the ocean. From behind, Mr. Robinson jumped on board the pinnace just as the wreck slipped away from the two rocks holding it and disappeared beneath the waves forever.

"That was a close one," said Mr. Robinson. He let out the sails of the pinnace and took hold of its rudder. "Let's head back, Fritz." The two returned to shore, Fritz in the casks, his father in the pinnace.

Mrs. Robinson and her three sons were waiting for them. The explosion had frightened them. And when they looked out and saw no sign of the wreck, they became even more alarmed. Relief came only when they saw the casks and a strange, small boat moving toward the shore.

On the beach, Fritz and his father were hugged by one and all. Then Mr. Robinson explained about the pinnace and how Fritz and he managed to get it free of the wreck.

"Well," said Mrs. Robinson, "Ernest, Jack, Franz, and I have not exactly been idle either."

She led her husband and oldest son back to Falconhurst. There, they saw a garden neatly laid out in rows. Beans, peas, potatoes, cabbages, and lettuce had been planted in a clearing of soil. And the salmon, herring, and rabbits hanging from a tree branch showed that the three younger boys had also been busy.

"Why, you've done wonders!" said Mr. Robinson joyfully.

That night was the happiest the family had spent on the island. They told each other of their day's adventures until fatigue eased them all into a deep sleep.

Days passed into weeks, then months. During that period, two more animals were added by the boys to their growing collection.

The first animal was found shortly after the boys discovered a gap in the cliffs. They walked through it and explored inland. Soon they came out onto a large, open plain where buffaloes grazed. They managed to capture a calf from the herd and return with it to Falconhurst.

Another time, Juno and Turk stumbled upon a large jackal guarding a crevice in the cliffs. The two dogs attacked and killed the jackal. Jack ran up behind them and, seeing the crevice, wedged his hand inside. When he pulled it out, he was holding a beautiful, golden-yellow baby jackal. It was no bigger than a housecat. The cub purred in Jack's arms as he cuddled it. And it took its place among the other animals tamed by the boys.

Not all creatures were welcome at Falconhurst, however. The tree the Robinsons were living in was also home to a swarm of bees. They had made their nest inside the trunk, entering and leaving through a small hole. In examining it, little Franz was stung on the nose. His yell brought Mrs. Robinson running. It was then decided to rid the tree of these pests. But how?

"We'll fill their hole with tobacco smoke," said Mr. Robinson. "And we'll stop up every other hole along the trunk with clay. They won't be able to escape the smoke, which will put them to sleep. Then all we have to do is collect them from inside, move them to a new nest, and plug up the hole again. We'll wait until dark. They should all be in their hole by then."

Evening came, and the Robinsons took gobs of wet clay and plugged up every hole they could find in the tree. Then Mr. Robinson cut a short piece of hollow bamboo and shoved it into the clay that filled the main hole. He stoked a tobacco pipe, filled his mouth with smoke, and blew it through the bamboo into the tree. He did this twice more, then capped the end of the bamboo with clay.

A tremendous buzzing sprang up within the tree. After a while, the buzzing died down. When not so much as a soft hum could be heard anymore, Mr. Robinson removed the bamboo and dug out the clay from the main hole. With a lit torch, he peered inside. There, motionless at the bottom of the hive, was a huge pile of slumbering bees.

The boys and their father carefully scooped out the sleeping bees and placed them in a new hive they prepared in a distant tree. Then Mr. Robinson filled in the main hole once more. It wasn't long before the bees awoke. Immediately, they flew from their new nest to their old one. But every hole was blocked with clay. They buzzed around and around the tree, clearly confused. The clay wouldn't budge from the holes. Finally, the bees returned to their new hive, leaving Falconhurst to the Robinsons.

Besides the honey they left behind, the bees provided another benefit. They showed the Robinsons that the tree was hollow inside. Mrs. Robinson had long complained about having to use the rope ladder. So her husband and sons decided to chip out the wood from the tree's center and build a stairway—inside!

Using the carpenter's tools from the wreck, the boys and their father hollowed out the inside hole even more. Then they took a strong sapling and anchored it in the middle at the bottom. Around it they nailed wooden slats, spiraling upward as they secured each one. When the top slat was flush with the tree house, Mr. Robinson cut a square opening in the tree. When he stepped out, he was standing on the plank floor of Falconhurst. Then it was a simple matter to fashion a door for the top of the stairs and a hatch door for the bottom. They could now climb up and down the tree easily. Mrs. Robinson would not have to use the rope ladder anymore.

Despite their hard work in making Falconhurst a safe, sturdy home, the Robinsons were driven down into the base of the tree trunk by the wind and rain of a winter storm. In these cramped quarters they stayed, trying to make the best of a bad situation. Outside, the rain poured and the wind whipped around the trunk. Above, they could hear the sailcloth roof of their tree house flapping.

Suddenly, there was a loud rip. Mr. Robinson scurried to the top of the stairs to see what it was. Opening the door, he saw that the sailcloth had been torn in half. Furniture had been knocked over, dishes were smashed, and everything was sopping wet from the rain. The Robinson family would now have to sit out the winter below with the supplies they managed to save. It wouldn't be easy. But they had no choice.

That first winter was all the reason the Robinsons needed to search for new lodgings. Living high in a tree was fine in the summer. Winter was another matter. They would have to find a shelter much better protected from the wind and rain. But what? Where?

"Father, remember that jackal killed by the dogs?" said Fritz. "It was guarding an opening in the cliffs. Maybe we could find one, too, or at least dig one out. Just for winter. Then we could come back to Falconhurst in the spring."

"A cave!" little Franz said excitedly. "Oh, Father, could we? It'd be such fun!"

"Hmm," said Mr. Robinson, rubbing his chin. "You may be right, Franz, though I doubt it'd be as much fun as you think. Dear?" He was now looking at his wife.

Mrs. Robinson glanced at her sons. Their eager faces convinced her. "All right, let's pack some supplies and look for our new winter home in the cliffs."

They set out the next morning. The buffalo pulled most of the supplies on a rough sled Mr. Robinson nailed together for the journey. With cow, donkey, ducks, geese, jackal, dogs, monkey, hens, and roosters, the Robinson family traveled past Tentholm and farther down the shoreline. When they came before a sheer, smooth rock face, Mr. Robinson signaled them to stop. He took out a pick and walked over to the base of the cliff. He swung. A piece of rock flew away. He swung again and another chip split off. Then the boys joined him. Soon picks, shovels, crowbars, hammers, and chisels were hacking furiously at the rock.

They camped right there on the beach. And for the next ten days, they dug, stopping only to eat and to sleep. Mrs. Robinson kept them fed and bandaged their blisters. The deeper they dug, the easier the rock broke away.

Suddenly, Jack shouted, "Gone, Father! Fritz, Ernest, Franz, look! My crowbar has gone through the mountain!"

"Run around and get it," said Fritz, laughing. "Perhaps it has dropped into Europe. You must not lose a good crowbar."

Jack failed to see the humor in any of this. "But really, it *fell* through. I heard it crash down inside."

"Crash?" said Mr. Robinson in surprise. He and his other three sons rushed to where Jack was standing. Mr. Robinson took a hammer and knocked some thin rock and soft dirt loose. The hole where Jack's crowbar fell through became wider. Mr. Robinson chipped away at the rock some more. It fell away easily. The boys helped him dig. Soon they had knocked out a hole large enough for Mr. Robinson to enter.

"Careful, boys," he warned. "If it is a cave, we don't know what may be inside."

Holding a pistol in one hand and a lit torch in the other, Mr. Robinson stepped through the hole. Suddenly, everything around him was ablaze. He shielded his eyes. Why, it was a vast cave of glittering crystal! Bright, golden light shone around and above him. Huge crystal pillars dangled from the ceiling and stood up from the hard-sand floor. Mr. Robinson rubbed his hand on one of these pillars and dabbed his finger to his tongue. Rock salt! He was standing in a cavern full of the best and purest salt!

"Boys," said their father from the cave opening, "go tell your mother we've found our winter home."

The days that followed were full of activity. Mrs. Robinson swept the sandy floor and dusted away the cobwebs. Sailcloth was used as a carpet. Tables, chairs, and bedding were moved inside. Window casings transported earlier from the wreck were placed in square holes dug into the outside wall. They now had windows!

From Falconhurst, Mr. Robinson and his sons removed the top door and carried it to the cave. There, they extended it and fitted it into place as their new front door. Fish caught from Jackal River were salted and stored away by their mother. It wasn't long at all before Rockburg, as the boys called it, was shaping up into a cozy winter home.

Fritz was putting a finishing touch to one of the windows when he saw something moving in the distance. It was coming from the direction of Jackal River.

"Father, Mother, come quick! There's something out there!" shouted Fritz.

The whole family looked through the windows. A light mist had rolled onto the beach, making it difficult to see far. But through it could be faintly seen a strange creature crawling along the sand—and heading for the cave.

"Quick!" ordered Mr. Robinson. "Help me put a plank across the front door, boys. And get your guns."

Then, the head of the creature rose up through the mist.

"A boa constrictor!" exclaimed Mr. Robinson. "And look at the size of it! Why, it must be at least thirty feet long!"

The snake continued its advance, writhing along the sand, occasionally rearing its head. It was obviously looking for its next meal. Mr. Robinson was determined it would not be his family. He stood ready with his gun loaded and cocked. Closer and closer came the huge snake. It coiled and uncoiled. Now it was no farther than thirty yards in front of the cave.

The boys could resist no longer. They opened fire at the snake from the windows. It ducked under the flying bullets and slithered back toward Jackal River. Seeing the creature retreat, the boys burst out the front door of Rockburg and chased after it, firing their guns. The snake was now heading toward Flamingo Marsh. As fast as the boys moved, the boa constrictor moved faster. It reached the marsh and slunk into the thick watery weeds before the boys could get there. The snake had escaped.

Unaware of the danger, the donkey broke free of its halter and galloped headlong into the marsh. In vain, the boys called after the donkey. Fritz was about to go into the marsh after it when his father firmly held him back. Then, about twenty yards into the marsh, the snake reared its head. Its dark, deadly jaws were open and its forked tongue darted out hungrily. With blinding speed, the boa constrictor struck, winding itself tightly around the startled donkey. The animal kicked and cried. But the struggle was useless. The snake's grip grew tighter and tighter on the donkey, squeezing the life out of it.

"Father, we can kill the snake from here!" screamed the boys. "Let us shoot it!"

"No," said Mr. Robinson. "You may hit the donkey, poor thing. It's too late now, anyway. We can't enter the marsh safely while the snake is in it."

The boys stared out at the marsh. They felt helpless as the donkey kicked its last and stiffened. In the tall, dense weeds of the marsh, nothing stirred.

"Our donkey is lost forever," said little Franz tearfully. "The snake has won."

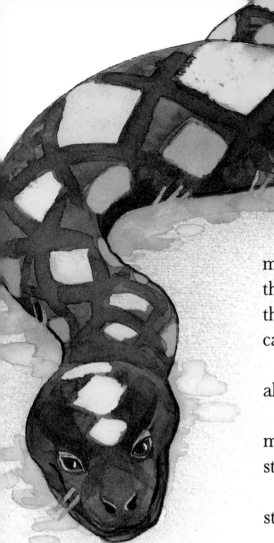

"No, not just yet, it hasn't," said Mr. Robinson. "It may have taken the donkey's life, but we shall soon take the snake's. Once it eats the donkey, it will be difficult for the snake to move and defend itself. And that's when we can get near enough to kill it."

"You don't mean that the snake will swallow the donkey all at once, do you, Father?" asked Jack, shocked.

"Snakes cannot chew their food, Jack. That's why they must swallow their prey whole. It then digests in their stomachs."

"But how can it swallow the *whole* donkey?" asked Jack, still not convinced.

"The boa constrictor will crush its prey's bones and body into a shapeless, soft mass. Slowly but surely, it will then grip the prey in its mouth and swallow it."

Many hours later, Jack noticed a long, black log lying on the grass at the edge of the marsh. A closer look told him it was not a log at all.

"Father, Fritz, Ernest, Franz, I've found the snake!" he shouted to the others.

Mr. Robinson and the three boys came running with their guns. Sure enough, the boa constrictor was lazing by the edge of the marsh. Its swollen belly and hooded eyes showed that it was now digesting its food. The snake glared at the Robinsons menacingly. Its movements, however, were slow and awkward.

That was all the invitation the boys and their father needed. They fired their guns together. The snake's tail lashed from side to side. Then, it stopped. The snake was dead.

Where *did* the boa constrictor come from? The only explanation Mr. Robinson could think of was the gap found by the boys in the cliffs. And so, taking a few supplies and guns, he decided to explore farther inland. Fritz, Ernest, Jack, and the two dogs accompanied him. Franz remained behind at the request of his mother.

As they walked through the gap, Mr. Robinson was proud of how well all his sons were turning out. They were truly a blessing to their parents. They had grown stronger and more mature, and each was a fine hunter. Mr. Robinson knew he could count on them in an emergency. This was especially true of his oldest son, Fritz. More and more, he was taking on responsibility for protecting the family and for guiding his brothers.

Just ahead lay the open plain. It was there that the boys had captured the buffalo calf several months ago. Mr. Robinson could see the herd roaming in the distance. Once past the plain, the four headed still farther inland. Soon they came to a desert where small clouds of dust could be seen far off.

"Father, I can see horsemen riding at full gallop toward us!" said Fritz.

Ernest and Jack nodded their heads in agreement. The idea of other humans on the island had them smiling in hope of a rescue. But Mr. Robinson, squinting hard to get a better look, shook his head.

"Boys, those horsemen you see are ostriches." He was pointing at the dust clouds, which were clearing. Fritz, Ernest, and Jack could now see that their father was right.

"Let's move along," said Mr. Robinson.

Ernest took the lead, trying to keep up with the two dogs ahead of him. The desert led into a wooded area. Then, Juno and Turk bolted off to the side into a thicket of tall bushes. A few minutes passed, then a yelp of terror arose from the bushes. Violent barking and vicious growling followed. Ernest ran after the dogs into the bushes. Within seconds, he emerged again.

"It's…it's…it's…" he stuttered in fear, trying to catch his breath.

"What?" asked Fritz. "Tell us!"

"A BEAR!" answered Ernest finally. "And it's coming this way!"

A moment later, a mammoth bear appeared. Then another bear, just as large and just as angry, sidled up next to it. Once together, the two enormous bears charged. Mr. Robinson and his three sons barely had time to aim their rifles and fire. In their haste to defend themselves, however, they only wounded the bears. It was then that the two dogs joined the fray. They leaped and snapped their jaws at the bears, circling around them just out of reach of their sharp claws.

Juno and Turk kept the bears busy as Mr. Robinson and the three boys advanced closer to them. They knew they couldn't fire their rifles again without risking injury to the dogs. They would have to shoot from close range, using pistols this time.

The bears saw them coming. But before the enraged beasts could lunge at the boys and their father, Fritz shot one through the head. It fell with a resounding thud to the ground, dead. The other bear, angrier still, was just about to spring at Fritz when Mr. Robinson, Ernest, and Jack opened fire with their pistols. The second bear crumpled to the earth, taking three bullets to the heart.

"Thank goodness!" cried Mr. Robinson. He jabbed the bears with his rifle barrel to make sure they were dead. Then he looked over at his three sons. They were still gawking at the dead bears. "You boys okay?" All three nodded.

Fritz spoke up first. "I guess we should skin them," he said, pulling out his knife. "Mother will be glad to replace her sailcloth carpet with a couple of bearskin rugs."

Together, the four made short work of it. The thick coats of the bears were removed, scraped, washed, salted, and dried. While the skins were drying in the sun, the meat was cut into sections. Then, ladened with dried skins and meat, the party of four returned across the desert, over the plain, through the gap, and home to Rockburg.

Ten years passed. The seasons seemed to tumble by quickly for the Robinson family. And throughout this period, Rockburg and Falconhurst remained their winter and summer homes.

Encouraged by his parents, Fritz became more and more independent. His father made a kayak for him so that he could explore the shore of the island alone. The kayak was made out of the skeleton of a whale, and bamboo canes were used to strengthen the sides and deck. Sealskin covered the whalebone and bamboo frame, making the craft light and watertight. Only a small, round hole was left on top. That was where Fritz sat and paddled. The kayak was modeled on those used by Eskimos and Greenlanders that Mr. Robinson had once read about.

Mr. Robinson understood his oldest son's restless nature. Fritz was twenty-five years old now. He was a full-grown man, able to take care of himself. He would often leave for hours in his kayak. Still, every time he did, Mrs. Robinson worried.

"Dear," she said to her husband, "are you sure that horrid soap bubble is safe enough for Fritz?" Ever since the first time she'd seen the kayak float, Mrs. Robinson had called it that. She was convinced it wasn't really seaworthy.

"Yes, I'm sure," replied her husband, smiling. "Why do you ask?"

"Well, it seems he's been away for far too long. Something could have happened to him."

"Don't worry, dear," said Mr. Robinson, taking her hand. "He knows what he's doing." But even as he tried to calm his wife's fear, Mr. Robinson silently wondered what had become of Fritz. He had been gone the entire day, and night was fast approaching.

Leaving his wife's side, Mr. Robinson walked down to the shoreline and gazed out on the water. He could barely make out Shark Island, let alone a kayak far off in the distance. But finally a small, black speck appeared on the horizon. It was slowly coming closer to shore. Then Mr. Robinson saw Fritz wave from the kayak, which was towing a large sack in the water. Fritz paddled the craft right up onto the beach where his father was standing.

"Welcome back, Fritz," said Mr. Robinson. "Your mother and I were beginning to worry about you."

"I'm sorry, Father," Fritz said as he untied the sack from behind the kayak and dragged it up onto the sand. "But ever since I got the kayak, I've been wanting to make a voyage farther along the coast. And now I have." His eyes gleamed. "Besides this walrus I killed, I made an interesting discovery. But let's get this sack back to Falconhurst right now. I'll tell you and the family what happened there."

Sitting up in the tree house, Fritz told his family about his adventure. He had traveled in the kayak past the outlying cliffs and rocks. Farther on, he passed still more cliffs, as well as shoals teeming with brightly colored fish. The waves were smooth and there was no wind to fight. It was a clear, sunny day.

He was beginning to enjoy himself when he saw water passing under a magnificent archway right into the side of a cliff. He paddled into the archway and realized it was the entrance to a vaulted cave that extended for hundreds of yards into the cliff. It emptied out into a bay surrounded on all sides by land. The water there was crystal clear. In it, Fritz could see thousands of oysters heaped on the bottom. Using his boat hook, he took up a number of them. When he cracked a few open, he found milky-white, pea-sized stones inside.

At this point in his story, Fritz took out a pouch and handed it to his mother. Untying the top, she spilled the contents onto a table.

"Pearls!" she exclaimed in awe. "Just look at them!"

Mr. Robinson, Ernest, Jack, and Franz bent over the table to get a better look. It was a dazzling sight!

Fritz resumed his story. After gathering up these pearls, he started to head back. But he came too close to the nest of some albatrosses. They screamed and wheeled over his head. When one swooped at him, Fritz took the boat hook and stunned it. He then managed to slip out of the bay and through the archway without further trouble.

On his way home to Falconhurst, he came across a walrus swimming nearby. He shot it and brought it back with him, knowing the walrus' skin would come in handy during the winter.

Ernest, Jack, and Franz oohed and aahed as Fritz spoke. Then the family once more settled down to a good night's sleep. They were all together again—and safe.

Next morning, before the others awoke, Fritz nudged his father and asked him to come outside. They climbed down the spiral stairway inside the tree and stepped out onto the beach. The sun's glinting rays were just then warming the cold sand under their feet.

"I left out one important part of my story last night, Father," whispered Fritz. "You probably thought I left the stunned albatross right where it fell in the water. But I didn't. I picked it up and examined it on the deck of the kayak. A piece of rag was curled around one of its legs. Imagine my shock when I unraveled it and read English words written on it. The words said, 'Save an unfortunate Englishwoman from the smoking rock!'

"I couldn't believe it. Was it possible another human being lived on the island? I replaced the piece of rag on the bird's leg. Then I tore part of my handkerchief and wrote on it, 'Don't give up hope! Help is near!' I wound my message around the albatross' other leg and then helped it to fly again. And off it flew, moving due west." Fritz looked at his father intently. "Father, do you think my note will reach this Englishwoman? Will I be able to find her? Save her? Bring her here?"

"Steady now, Fritz," replied his father in a low voice. "Don't jump to conclusions. You don't know when the note was written. It could have been years ago. The person who wrote it may be dead. And you can't be sure it was written by someone on this island. There are hundreds of small islands around here. The albatross carrying the note could have come from any of them."

"What about the smoking rock?" asked Fritz.

"That probably means an active volcano," answered his father. "But there are no active volcanos in these waters."

Fritz dropped his head. Then he looked up at his father again. Mr. Robinson realized his son wouldn't give up without one more try.

"Let's have breakfast with the others, Fritz," he said. "Afterward, you can take the kayak out again. Before you do, though, make sure it can carry *two* people." Mr. Robinson winked at his son. "Just in case you find her. But not a word of the Englishwoman's note to the others. I don't want to get their hopes up falsely. Okay?"

"Yes," said Fritz, smiling.

Right after breakfast, Fritz took the kayak out to sea once more. The rest of the family waved as he paddled out of view.

Five days went by and Fritz did not return. This was by far the longest period he'd been away. The entire family was worried, especially his mother.

"Something happened," she said to her husband. "I just know it. We must go after him. Please."

At sunrise the next day, Mr. Robinson got the pinnace ready for the trip. All the Robinsons insisted on going. After stowing some supplies on board, they sailed out in calm, clear weather. Fritz's story was still fresh in their minds, so they had no trouble finding their way. They rounded the cliffs, passed another outcropping, and finally saw the archway. Heading through it, they came out onto the bay. Below, large beds of oysters could plainly be seen. And in the distance, they could see the outline of the kayak. It was Fritz!

The two boats were soon side by side. When Fritz boarded the pinnace, his mother hugged him. Mr. Robinson shook his hand and clapped him on the back. Fritz's brothers did the same.

"Fritz," said his mother, wiping a happy tear from her cheek, "what on earth happened to you? We were worried sick."

"If you'll follow me in the pinnace, I'll show you," he replied. The look Fritz gave his father told him the English-woman had been found alive.

Fritz sprang into his kayak and led the pinnace to a beautiful little island in the bay. During this short trip, Mr. Robinson told his wife and three sons about the note Fritz had found.

Mrs. Robinson was a little annoyed. "Why didn't you tell us from the start?" she asked.

"I didn't want to raise your hopes and then see them dashed," her husband replied. "I had to be sure. And now I am."

In the distance, smoke rose from atop a high, rocky cliff. It was the smoking rock mentioned in the note! Beaching the pinnace just below the cliff, the family followed Fritz in the direction of a hut. It was made of sheltering boughs, and a small fire burned in front of it. Fritz entered the hut. A moment later, he came out, leading a young woman by the hand.

"This is Jenny Montrose," said Fritz. "Like us, she was shipwrecked. She's been living here for three years."

Mrs. Robinson rushed over and gave her a warm hug. Mr. Robinson shook her hand. But the three boys stayed back. They were unsure how to act. Apart from their mother, they hadn't seen a woman in over ten years. Then Jenny smiled at them and shook each one's hand. Together, Ernest, Jack, and Franz let out three cheers for their new-found sister.

Fritz then told his family how he had sighted the fire on the cliff and found Jenny keeping it aflame. It was a beacon to any ship that might see it and rescue her.

Jenny herself then told the Robinsons how she was shipwrecked. Her father, a British colonel serving in India, had sent her on the ship *Dorcas* that was going to England. The colonel hoped to join his daughter there once his tour of duty in Calcutta was complete. But the *Dorcas* was swept off course by a violent storm and crashed into some rocks. The lifeboat carrying Jenny and the crew capsized. She was the only one to make it safely to shore.

43

There, she had lived for the past three years. In that time, she had built the hut. She had also tamed some albatrosses and used them to carry her messages for help. And each day without fail, she rekindled the fire on top of the cliff.

"But why didn't you return to us with Jenny immediately, Fritz?" asked his father.

"The skin of the kayak was damaged by some rocks offshore," said Fritz. "I had just finished patching her up and was taking her out to test her when you arrived. Believe me, I'll be glad to get back to Falconhurst."

"There's still plenty of daylight left," said Mr. Robinson, looking up at the sun. "Jenny, would you be our guest? I think you'll find Falconhurst and Rockburg a bit more to your liking than here."

Without delay, Jenny packed her belongings and joined the Robinsons in their journey to the other end of the island. She lived among them as the sister and daughter they never had. She laughed and raced with the boys on the beach during the rest of the summer in Falconhurst. And she spent long, quiet evenings sewing and weaving with Mrs. Robinson during the winter in Rockburg.

Mr. and Mrs. Robinson noticed a change in the behavior of their oldest son. Fritz helped Jenny carry things and saw to it that she was always comfortable. When spring came again, they took long walks together along the shore.

One day, as the two peered across the sea, they heard three booming sounds coming from far away. The rest of the family heard the sounds, too. They all came racing down from Falconhurst and, standing by Fritz and Jenny, squinted out over the water. Barely a dot on the distant waves, a flag fluttered in the breeze. There could be no mistake. It was a ship!

"Quick, Fritz," cried Mr. Robinson, "fire the two guns of the pinnace." Fritz leaped into the pinnace, which was anchored a few yards away, and jubilantly fired the guns. From the distance, two more shots could be heard in reply.

"We're saved!" shouted Franz. "Saved!"

It was a British brig of war, and the captain and some of his crew came ashore in a boat. They were dumbfounded by the sight of five men and two women greeting them with open arms. The tree house of Falconhurst and the cave home of Rockburg surprised them even more.

The Robinsons and Jenny quickly told the captain their stories. His eyes widened in amazement as each adventure was told. He then told them of his own mission—to find Jenny Montrose. Colonel Montrose never gave up hope of finding his daughter. For the past three years, he had searched for Jenny, and he commissioned other ships to search for her as well. The captain's ship was one of them.

''My mission is now over,'' he said with a smile. ''I've found Colonel Montrose's daughter. And happily, I've found all of you, too.'' He was looking at the Robinsons, who beamed back at him. ''Gather your belongings. First light tomorrow, we'll return for you. Then, it's off to England!''

The captain shook hands with everyone and said goodbye. After he returned to his ship, the Robinsons and Jenny celebrated their rescue with a lavish feast. As they sat there eating, each one suddenly realized that the years of waiting, hoping, and praying were over. They had been saved. They could now leave the island. Yet not everyone looked happy.

Mr. Robinson leaned over to his wife and whispered something in her ear. She whispered back. Then he spoke to his sons. "Your mother and I have decided to remain on the island. We've grown to love it here and have no desire to leave. But we will go if all of you want to."

"I'd like to go with Jenny to England," said Fritz. He and Jenny shared a quick, knowing glance.

Ernest and Jack looked at each other and silently nodded. "Jack and I would like to stay here with Father and Mother," said Ernest softly. Mr. and Mrs. Robinson smiled proudly at the two of them.

Then, everyone looked at Franz.

"If Fritz and Jenny don't mind," said Franz, "I'd like to go with them to England. From there, I can travel to Switzerland. I'd like to take up a career there. Besides, one of us ought to go home again, don't you think?" His parents nodded their consent, as did his brothers. "I love you all. And I promise to return for visits here at...at... Say, Father, we never did get around to naming this island. What should we call it?"

"In honor of your eventual return home, Franz," said his father, "how about 'New Switzerland'?"

"Hooray for New Switzerland!" shouted the family and Jenny together.

Good food, good cheer, and just being together made all their spirits soar that night. And as each one lay in bed waiting for sleep, one thought was shared by all. No matter how far or how long they might live apart, nothing would break up this family. Ever.